The Ren Faire Murders

Auriga Books

The Ren Faire Murders

Cal Rydell

Auriga Books

The Ren Faire Murders

Published in the United States by:
Auriga Books

First Edition
ISBN 978-0-9839850-5-1

To Kevin and Mike,
with many thanks for your
expert assistance

Contents

Chapter One

I was sitting at my laptop, making some final changes on my latest young adult book—a book about the 1960s in a ten-book series about the twentieth century—when I heard a knock at the front door. I clicked the "save" icon in the upper left corner of the page, closed the document, and got up to answer the door. I always close my documents when I stop working because I like to know how much time I've spent on them. Even when I answer the phone, I close the document so MS Word, which keeps a running count of a document's editing time, isn't creating a false profile of my work. A police officer and man in a dark suit were standing outside.

"Good afternoon," said the officer. "Are you Mark Rydberg?"

"Yes," I said. "Can I help you?"

"I hope so. My name is Officer Dawkins. I'm with the Norwalk Police Department. This is Detective Brenner, from the Minneapolis Police Department."

Brenner held out his badge for me to inspect.

"I see. What can I do for you?"

"I would like to ask you some questions," said Brenner.

"Okay. Would you like to come inside?"

"Would you be willing to come down to the station with us? That's routine procedure."

"I suppose so. When would you like me to do it?"

"Right now, if it's convenient."

"How long will it take?"

"Not too long. Maybe an hour or so."

"My wife gets off work at six. She doesn't drive, so I have to be there to pick her up."

"That's fine. It gives us all afternoon."

"Do I have to go with you, or can I drive there myself?"

"You can drive," said Dawkins. "What kind of car do you have?"

"A Toyota pick-up."

"No problem. Just follow me to the station."

"Sure. Let me get my wallet."

I went back to the bedroom and grabbed my wallet, phone, and eyeglasses. I quickly put on a clean shirt—my favorite red polo shirt. I made a quick stop in the bathroom so I wouldn't have to use the one at the station. I was out the front door in less than five minutes. Brenner was standing beside a grey Ford Police Interceptor utility vehicle.

"My truck's behind the security gate," I said, pointing to the black gate at the end of the driveway.

I started my truck, made the tight left turn through the security gate, and began to follow the police car down the long driveway that led to the street my apartment complex faced. All I could think about was what I would tell Luz, my wife, if I wasn't back in time to pick her up. I knew she would panic as soon as she heard the word *pulis*, as they say it in her native country, the Philippines. All I could hope was that I could clear things up before she got off work.

When we got to the station, Dawkins and Brenner led me to a small room with a table, three chairs, and a camera above the door. It looked exactly like those interrogation rooms you see on YouTube.

"Have a seat," said Brenner, motioning toward a chair. Fortunately, it was a living-room-style chair, not one of those hard metal chairs. I've always had lower back pain, and my back was already hurting.

"Would you like something to drink?"

"What do you have?"

"Coffee. Tea. Soda. Water."

"Is this one of those things where you're going to save the cup to get my DNA?"

"What do you mean?"

"Never mind. I'm okay."

"Nothing to drink?"

"No, thanks." I knew if I drank anything, I would have to pee, and that would just add to my anxiety.

Brenner nodded to Dawkins, and the officer left the room, closing the door behind him. Brenner appeared to be in his forties, which looked young to me. When you're seventy, every authority figure looks surprisingly young. I remember the first time I had a doctor who was younger than I was. It was the first time I noticed that I was approaching middle age, or perhaps had already arrived.

Brenner sat down at the table and opened his notebook.

"Tell me a little about yourself," he said.

"Like what?"

"What do you do for a living?"

"I'm a writer. I was an advertising copywriter for about forty years. I still do a little consulting. But I also write books. I've published two novels."

"That must be interesting."

"It's interesting for me, but from the outside, it's pretty boring. All I do is sit in one place and type. A writer is never happier than when he or she is alone in a room for hours on end."

"I suppose that's right. Now, where are you from? Did you grow up here?"

"I grew up in the Valley, actually. I graduated from Canoga Park High. But I was born in Iowa and lived in

Phoenix from the age of two until I was ten. Then we moved to California."

"Have you lived anywhere else?"

"Oh, man. I've lived all over the place."

"Like where?"

"I went to college in Minnesota and ended up living there for about fifteen years. Then I moved to San Diego. I was there for twenty-odd years. I worked abroad. I was in Abu Dhabi, for four years. I met my wife there. She's from the Philippines.

"When my contract was up in Abu Dhabi, we moved to the Philippines and got married. I was there for five years. We have a house there. We came to the USA, let's see, seven years ago. We were in Northern California for a while, and now we're here."

"That's quite a history. Why did you come back to the US?"

"My brother passed away, and all of my belongings were in storage at his house. His widow sold the house, and she needed me to get my stuff. My wife came with me. We stayed with friends we made in the Philippines—an American guy and his Filipina wife.

"My wife decided she wanted to try working here. She got a temporary work permit, then a green card, and now we're here. For me, it's like coming home. This part of Los Angeles is a lot like the Valley."

"What did you do in Minnesota?"

"Like I said, I went to college there, but I dropped out after a year. My girlfriend at the time applied to the same school I went to and got a full scholarship. We lived together while she was in school. I worked at a place that made hats and caps."

"Really?"

"Yeah. It was interesting work. I had to join the union. Believe it or not, I was a member of the Ladies Garment Workers Union."

"How long did you do that?"

"I was there for five years. Eventually, I was laid off. I applied for a job as an advertising copywriter and was fortunate enough to get it. When my girlfriend graduated from college, we got married, bought a house in Saint Paul, and had a couple kids."

"Were you writing novels back then?"

"No. I was writing poetry."

"So, you've always been a writer?"

"Yes. I wrote my first published poem when I was in high school. My teacher thought it was publishable, so he taught me how to submit my work for publication. I had never seen myself as a writer before that, but he treated me like a professional. I've been at it ever since."

"What years were you in Minnesota?"

“Let’s see. I went to college there in 1973–1974. I returned with my girlfriend in 1976. We were there until 1988.”

“When you were there, did you hear about a string of murders involving young women?”

I paused to think. “No, I don’t remember that. But I’m not surprised. I call it my Black Hole period.”

“You mean drugs and alcohol?”

“Oh, no. Nothing like that. But when I moved there, I didn’t know any of the radio stations and I couldn’t find one I liked, so I didn’t listen to the radio. I didn’t have a TV. And I was so busy with schoolwork that I never read the newspapers or magazines. I completely lost touch with popular culture. When my girlfriend and I moved there, she was in college with a heavy workload. So we never had a TV or listened to anything except classical music. I remember when I played trivia games with friends years later, I could answer anything before 1973 and after 1981, when our first child was born, because we got a TV then. But the rest of the Seventies is a black hole. I remember we were in a café once, and a radio was playing in the kitchen. I could barely hear it, but I heard so-and-so won Wimbledon for the fifth time. I thought to myself, ‘Wow, Jimmy Connors has won Wimbledon five times.’ But I later learned it wasn’t Connors. It was Bjorn Borg. I had never heard of Bjorn Borg.”

"I see." Brenner made a note. "They called the killings the Ren Faire murders."

"Ren Faire?"

"Yes."

"What year was that?"

"1978."

"1978? Are you sure?"

"Yes. Why?"

"Well, at about that time, I worked at the Renaissance Festival in Shakopee."

"Really? What did you do?"

"It's kind of a long story."

"That's okay."

"At the time, I was working at the hat factory and writing a lot of poetry. I tried to write every day. A friend of my girlfriend, a girl named Lisa, was an artist. She had made a batik of a horse with rain coming off its mane and tail. She called it the storm horse. I wrote a poem about it, and then I wrote a whole series of poems about mythical horses to go with the four ancient elements—earth, water, air, and fire. 'The Earth Horse,' 'The Surf Horse,' 'The Storm Horse,' and 'The Horse of Fire.'"

"Like the Chinese New Year animal."

"I know, right? I was surprised to see the horse of fire is a Chinese symbol. Anyway, Lisa and I decided to put together a pamphlet of poetry and artwork and try to sell it at the Renaissance Festival. I had a friend copy out my poems in calligraphy, and Lisa did pen-and-ink drawings, which, when they were printed, she water-colored by hand—in the style of William Blake's *Songs of Innocence and Experience*. Even though the pamphlet was press-printed, and thus anachronistic, they let us sell it at the Renaissance Festival."

"And this was 1978?"

"I think so. '77 or '78."

"But you never heard about any murders there?"

"No, I didn't."

"Did you meet anyone there?"

"What do you mean?"

"Did you meet any women?"

This felt awkward. It seemed like Brenner knew more than he was letting on. I got the distinct impression that he was driving at something. I figured I'd better answer truthfully.

"Yes."

"Can you tell me about that?"

"Is it important?"

"It could be."

This worried me. "Am I in trouble?"

"Not that I know of."

"Well, why all these questions about the Renaissance Festival?"

"We're working on a cold case and we're just trying to collect as much information as we can. A couple of the victims worked at the Renaissance Festival."

"So you already knew that I had worked there?"

"Yes, we heard something about it, so I figured I would ask you."

"So you've already been investigating me."

"We've been investigating the case, interviewing anyone who might have been there. Your name came up. Why do you think we knocked on your door? We didn't pick your name out of the phone book."

I wondered who they had been talking to. There were only three possibilities: Lisa, my Renaissance Festival collaborator; Diane, my ex-wife; and possibly Cheryl, my old college girlfriend. I met a couple of her friends at the faire one time, and they gave me a ride home at the end of the day.

"What do you want to know?"

"Tell me everything you can. Who did you meet there?"

"Honestly, I only knew them by their first names. Who knows? They might have been pseudonyms."

"Why do you say that?"

"Well, everyone at the Ren Faire is playing a part. We're putting on a show for the public. We're speaking with fake British accents and even using Shakespearean words like 'thee' and 'thou.' The girls might have been using made-up names, like stage names."

Brenner made a note. "Please go on. What do you recall?"

"This is just between us, right?"

"What do you mean?"

"I mean, it's not something you're going to tell my wife or, I don't know, publish online."

"No. This is for the investigation only."

"All right. One of the girls said her name was Colleen. She had bright red hair and was very pretty. A little overweight, but lovely. She was a paid actress, interacting with the crowd to contribute to the festive atmosphere. She played a wench."

"A wench?"

"That's what she told me. She was wearing a low-cut peasant blouse and a tight-fitting bodice that pushed her breasts up and together. She was being flirty with me—and I guess with everyone. She came by several times, chatting me up, showing off her cleavage, saying naughty things. She was good at it. I figured it was all an act."

"Go on."

"Well, I was wearing this horrendous costume. I had wanted to dress like Shakespeare or Sir Walter Raleigh, with a doublet or whatever it's called, but I didn't have the money to buy a proper costume or have one made.

"My girlfriend, Diane, bought some muslin fabric and made a loose-fitting robe for me. She said I could play a wandering poet. But the robe looked medieval, not Renaissance. It was cheap and drab. I hated it. I mean, it felt like I was wearing a dress—not that I've ever worn one—but it was open at the bottom, you know? When I walked, I could feel the air coming up to my crotch—something a guy never feels. I felt ridiculous in it."

"I imagine that was a strange feeling."

"Exactly. Now that I think about it, Diane probably wanted me to feel ridiculous. She didn't want me to take part in the Ren Faire in the first place. She only agreed because Lisa was her best friend. Lisa had always wanted to be in the festival. Diane agreed to help Lisa by making my costume. I'll bet she secretly wanted me to look like crap. She made me a dress to humiliate me, to emasculate me, so I wouldn't flirt with other women."

"Did you flirt with Colleen?"

"Not exactly. I was getting to that. You see, this stupid robe I was wearing was loose, and Colleen came up to me, took me by the arm, and was coming on to me, right? She was pressing her breast against my arm and doing a kind of bump-and-grind against my leg, sort of dry-humping it. Not for just a second, either. She was doing it for quite a while, all the time looking up at me and talking dirty.

"Now, mind you, I was only twenty-three at the time, and my body started to, you know, react. I'm wearing this stupid robe so there's nothing to hide my reaction. So I say: 'Is there someplace we can go?' She says: 'Aye, my handsome poet,' and leads me by the hand. We walk past the vendor booths, across a meadow where they held jousting and swordfights, all the way to a nearby knoll or hill. We go over the crest of the hill so we're out of sight. The hill is covered with tall grass. She sits down on her skirt, leans back, and pulls the front of her skirt up to her waist. She wasn't wearing any underwear. I remember she had bright red pubic hair. I had never seen red pubic hair—well, maybe in the showers in school. All the boys used to shower together after PE back then. So I guess I had seen red pubic hair, but not on a girl. I remember kneeling on her skirt and looking around. No one could see us. I leaned over her, and we started kissing. She was a great kisser. It's strange. I don't remember if I took off my robe or just pulled it up. I probably took it off, but I don't remember being completely naked in the daylight. Regardless, we made love there on the hillside, beneath the summer sun. It was really beautiful, actually. I didn't use a condom. This was back in the days before STDs were common. There wasn't any AIDS yet, and hardly anyone used protection. I asked her if she used birth control, and she said yes, so I, um, you know..."

"You ejaculated inside her?"

"Yes."

"Then what happened?"

"Let's see. That's a little foggy to me. I actually have no recollection of coming down off that hill together with her. I'm pretty sure I did, though. I mean, I wouldn't have just gotten up and left her. That wouldn't have been right. I know that I eventually went back to the place where I had been selling my pamphlets, but I don't remember if she accompanied me there."

"Did you see her again?"

I looked down, trying hard to remember. Nothing came to me. "I have no recollection of seeing her after our encounter. I probably did. I worked there a couple more weekends. I just don't remember it. We parted on good terms, but we never renewed our sexual relationship. At least, I don't think we did.

"As I've gotten older, I've noticed that some memories have disappeared. I've been reminded of things that happened, by people I have every reason to believe, but I have no recollection of them at all. I've always had great recall. There are a lot of things that I remember that my friends and former classmates have forgotten. But lately I've realized that my memory is not what it used to be."

"Did you see her that night, after the festival closed?"

"No. I don't think so. Most of the Ren Faire people stayed there overnight. They would eat together and they would have a big bonfire. They would party all night and who knows what all. It seemed that Colleen was part of that crowd. I have no real reason to say that, other than that she seemed very comfortable there—she knew a lot of the other workers.

"I wanted to stay overnight, but Diane wanted me to come home every night. She didn't trust me staying away overnight. Well, I guess you can see why.

"Lisa spent Saturday nights there. She had a pup tent. She even invited me to stay with her. It probably would have made her feel a little safer. But Diane insisted that I come home every night.

"That was a real hassle, too, because I didn't have a car at the time, and Shakopee was at least an hour away from where I lived in St. Paul. But Diane didn't care. She didn't care how much she inconvenienced others—especially me. She just gave orders like a little Hitler.

"On Sundays, I usually got a ride back with Lisa. But on Saturdays, I had to hitchhike. That was back when people still did that. It was dying out, but Ren Faire folks were pretty open to giving rides. If I could get to anywhere in the Twin Cities, I could take a bus home. I always had a bus pass.

"Did Colleen give you a ride that night?"

"No, I told you—I didn't see her after our escapade on the hill. That's another weird thing I just thought of. Just thinking about hitchhiking back and forth... I'm sure I only wore that stupid costume at the festival. I wore street clothes going there and coming back. So I must've brought something to carry the costume in. And the pamphlets I sold. And a place to stash my street clothes once I got there. But I have no memory of carrying a knapsack or any kind of bag."

"So you believe you hitchhiked home the night you had sex with Colleen?"

"If it was a Saturday, yes. If it was a Sunday, then I might've gotten a ride with Lisa. There's only one time I didn't go home on a Saturday night."

"When was that?"

Chapter Two

"I don't know the exact date. I don't know the dates of any of this. You'd have to look them up—or maybe you already have. Anyway, one Saturday it started raining. Typical Minnesota summer. I lived there for fifteen years, but I never got used to the way it rained in the summer. I was a California kid through and through, but I had gotten the idea that colleges were better in the East and Midwest, so I ended up going to Hamline University in Saint Paul. I hated summers there—the humidity, the mosquitoes, the rain. I actually preferred the winters. It was cold, but at least it was sunny. And all the bugs were dead.

"I couldn't get out of Minnesota soon enough. When I got back to California, I met Diane when she was in high school. She also went to Canoga Park High, and my old creative writing teacher—the one who got me thinking about writing as a profession—introduced us. I told her what a great school Hamline was. She applied and got a full scholarship. We decided to live together in Minnesota. I hated to go back, but, you know, I figured it would only be while she was in college.

"Anyway, back to the story. One Saturday night it was raining hard. Buckets, as the locals used to say. There was no way I could get a ride home. I remember talking to Lisa about it. She said I could stay in her tent. I thanked her, but I said no."

"Why?"

"Diane would have had a shit-fit if I'd stayed in Lisa's tent. She was insanely jealous. Even if it was her best friend—someone she should trust—she wouldn't want us to spend the night together. As I said before, I can understand why. I was a bit of a horndog. Besides, Lisa was beautiful and had a great body. I say that with confidence, not because I ever slept with her, but because her parents had a hot tub, and one time when they were out of town, she invited a few of us over. We all got naked in the hot tub.

"Lisa looked amazing. Diane was furious with me because I kept looking at Lisa. What could I do? She was sitting right across from me, and we were all talking, trying to be cool, like we didn't even notice we were naked—but of course I noticed. Anyway, I wouldn't have trusted myself alone all night with her, either."

"So what did you do?"

"Well, that's the thing. That's why I remember it so well. I was hanging out by one of the vendor booths, just trying to stay out of the rain. I started talking to this dark-haired girl who was wearing a sort of woven, fishnet-like dress. I can't remember if it was see-through or had some kind of lining. I seem to remember it was see-through, but that would have been pretty risqué, even for a Renaissance Festival. It had long, tight sleeves and was tight everywhere—kind of like something Elvira might wear, or Morticia from *The Addams Family*, but burgundy, not black. Tight, with a plunging neckline. She looked great in it. Flawless figure. Beautiful skin. She was way out of my league, to be honest. Anyway, she asked where I was staying, and I said I had no idea. She said she was going to spend the night in the booth—I guess she worked there. She said I could stay there too, if I wanted."

"Go on."

"Well, you're probably getting the picture by now. I stayed, and we had sex. I don't remember it clearly. It was dark—no electricity out there. I don't think we had a flashlight or lantern. Maybe candles. I remember seeing her a little, so it wasn't pitch black. She didn't take her dress all the way off. She lifted it from the bottom when we had sex. I don't even remember what position we were in. I don't remember anything about it, actually. It probably didn't last very long. I came pretty fast back then, especially the first time I was with someone—especially someone as beautiful as she was.

"But I know for sure that we did it. I kept count, you know. She and Colleen were on my 'list.' I've thought of her many times. She was breathtaking. Her name was Deborah."

"And did you see Deborah again?"

I paused to think. Most of the memories were gone. The sexual encounters were clear—probably because I'd gone over them in my mind—but the rest was hazy.

"Not that I remember. Her booth was near where I usually sold my pamphlets, so I probably saw her in passing, but I don't recall speaking to her or anything."

"All right, Mr. Rydberg. May I call you Mark?"

"Sure."

"All right, Mark, I'm going to step out for a moment. I'll be right back."

"Could you bring me a cup of coffee when you come back?"

"Sure."

As Brenner left, I glanced up at the camera. They were taping this. I wondered if anyone else had been watching. I thought about what I'd said. They always say not to volunteer anything to the police, but I hadn't said anything incriminating, I didn't think. Maybe I'd bragged a little, but everything I'd said was true. I hoped Brenner would come back and tell me I could go.

Chapter Three

Brenner returned in about five minutes. A woman followed him into the room.

"Mark," said Brenner, "this is Lieutenant Thorsen."

I stood up and shook her hand. I made a point of not making a noise when I stood. I remember hearing a celebrity—I think it was Peter Asher of the duo Peter and Gordon—say that the only advice his father ever gave him was not to make an involuntary noise when he stood up or sat down. Once I was made aware of it, I realized I had been grunting or sighing whenever I stood or sat, and it made me seem old—older than I felt. No more of that, especially not in front of the police.

"Nice to meet you," I said, "although I wish it was under different circumstances."

"I do, too, Mr. Rydberg."

"You can call me Mark. Lieutenant Brenner, here, does."

"All right, Mr. Rydberg."

So this was the good cop/bad cop routine. They must really be after something.

Brenner placed a cup of coffee on the corner of the table, within my reach. I picked it up and took a sip. Coffee is almost never too hot for me. The hotter the better.

“This is good stuff,” I said. I took another sip and set the cup down. I took a good look at Lieutenant Thorsen. Her face was pretty. Hazel eyes. Delicate nose. Shapely lips. I estimated she was in her mid-thirties. Her prime. I remember going to my twentieth high school reunion. The women were all thirty-seven or thirty-eight, and they looked amazing—so much better than they did in high school. I think the late thirties is the peak for feminine beauty.

“Lieutenant Brenner has briefed me on what you’ve said,” Thorsen said. She sat down at the table across from Brenner, opened a binder, and took out a photograph. She handed it to me. “Do you know this woman?”

I put on my +1.50, plastic reading glasses from the Dollar Tree store and took a look. The picture was of a pretty, young redhead with freckles across her nose. Her face was roundish, as if she were a little overweight. I assumed it was Colleen, but I answered truthfully: “I can’t say for sure. It’s not anyone I’ve met in the last twenty or thirty years, I don’t think.”

“This would have been before that. She was last seen alive in 1978.”

“She’s dead?”

“Yes.”

Tears welled up in my eyes. The date confirmed my hunch, and it hurt to think that this beautiful young woman who had once touched my life had lost her own. I've always gotten choked up easily, but the older I've gotten, the more quickly tears come. I took a deep breath and tried to compose myself.

"Is it Colleen, from the Renaissance Festival?"

"That's right. Colleen Malone."

Hearing her last name made it even more real. "Colleen Malone. I never knew her last name. It's sad to think she's gone. She was so beautiful, so funny, so full of life."

"Yes."

"She died in 1978?"

Thorsen nodded.

"How did she die?"

"That's what we were hoping you would help us with."

"Me? Why me?" I said, still wrestling with my emotions. I took off my glasses and wiped my eyes. "I'm sorry. It's just that this is a shock. I mean, I guess it's been about fifty years since it happened, but I'm just finding out now, you know. I'm sure you understand."

"We're asking you because we recently ran some tests on semen that was taken from her body after her death. We ran the DNA through a genealogical database. The DNA is a close match to yours—close enough to bring you in for questioning.

If you consent to a buccal swab, we'll test your DNA to see it's an exact match."

"Or not."

"Or not," Thorsen agreed.

I suspected they had already collected my DNA from my trash or another source. I had read about such cases.

"All right."

"You're consenting to a buccal swab?"

"Sure. Why not? You probably have a sample of my DNA already, or you'll have one soon from the coffee cup."

Brenner opened the door and called down the hallway. A minute later, a female officer entered the room holding a glass tube and a swab in paper wrapping.

"I hope this isn't as uncomfortable as a COVID test," I said.

She smiled, as I had hoped.

After she left, Thorsen resumed her questioning.

"You admit that you had sex with Colleen Malone shortly before her death."

"Hold on. I said I had sex with her. I have no idea when she died."

"Your semen was still inside her, so it was soon afterward."

"Okay. But I asked you how she died, and you never answered."

"Do you know?"

"No, I don't. But with all of this talk about DNA, I'm beginning to suspect foul play."

"That's right. She was murdered."

"That's terrible," I managed to whisper. Again, tears clouded my eyes.

"As far as we know, you were the last person to see her alive."

"You think I killed her?" I asked, wiping the tears from my eyes.

"Did you?"

"No, I didn't."

"Do you know who might have? Did you see anyone with her?"

"No, I don't have any idea. She played the part of a wench and flirted with a lot of guys—that was her role at the faire—but I don't remember anything specific."

Thorsen took another photo out of her binder and handed it to me. "Do you know this woman?"

I put on my glasses. It looked like Deborah: dark hair, pale skin, bewitching.

"Wait a minute," I said. "What is going on here? Is this some kind of sick joke?"

Thorsen just looked at me.

"Come on! Are you guys pranking me? This can't be real. Is this a TV show or something?" I could hear my voice rising, but I couldn't help it.

"Calm down, Mr. Rydberg."

"Calm down? Are you fucking kidding me? Are you trying to tell me that Deb is dead, and that you have my DNA on her, too?"

"Is she dead?"

"How the fuck would I know? But why are you pulling out her picture? What the fuck?"

"Calm down, Mark," said Brenner. "This all happened a long time ago. It must be a tremendous burden for you to bear. Why don't you tell us what happened."

I looked at the picture and tried to process what was going on. It felt like a nightmare—one where you're trapped and can't wake yourself up. My heart was pounding and my vision was pulsating. I took a deep breath.

"Let me get this straight," I said. "Two young women—two young women I had sex with at the Renaissance Festival—are dead. And you think I killed them because you found my DNA on both of them."

"That's why we're talking with you, Mr. Rydberg," said Thorsen. "You admit you were with them shortly before they died."

"Yeah, but I never said I killed them."

"Did you kill them?"

"No, I didn't! I didn't even know they were dead. They were two beautiful girls from a great time in my life—a time when life was simpler, and we were young and free. They were two girls who gave me memories I've cherished all my life. But that's all there is to it. I didn't kill them. They were both alive when I saw them last."

"All right, Mr. Rydberg. Is there anyone who can verify your story?"

"What do you mean?"

"Let's start with Deborah Jorgenson. You say you spent the night with her in a vendor booth at the Renaissance Festival. Can anyone verify that?"

"Now? Fifty years later?"

"Yes."

"No. I mean, I saw Lisa the next morning—Lisa Grossman, a friend of my ex-wife who was working with me at the faire—and told her where I'd stayed. I didn't tell her who I stayed with. I talked to her to make sure she'd corroborate my story when I told Diane why I didn't come home the night before. I was hoping Lisa would help stop a fight before it started. She'd confirm it was raining hard, and that's why I didn't get a ride home. She'd also confirm I didn't spend the night with her. I knew Diane would be in a rage because I didn't come home.

Maybe Lisa remembers me spending the night there, and she could corroborate my story."

"But no one saw you in the booth any time that night?"

"Only Deb, and even that is a little hazy."

"What do you mean?"

"I mean I don't have a memory of sleeping in the booth or waking up with her. I don't remember any of that. I barely remember having sex with her."

"Did you go home with her?"

"No, I told you, I spent the night in the booth."

"But you're not sure about that."

"Well... no."

"No one saw you there?"

"No. Not that I know of."

"Did you get in a fight with her?"

"What? No."

"Did she say something to make you angry? Did you fly into a rage with her, like you just did here?"

"Look, Lieutenant, you're hitting me with some heavy shit here. Of course I'm going to react. You're accusing me of something terrible. And let's face it—you're being sneaky about it. You're trying to trap me into saying something you can use against me."

"I'm just asking questions."

"Bullshit. You're fucking toying with me. Well, go ahead and fuck with me. I have nothing to hide. Maybe I'm a Lothario, maybe I'm Don Juan, but I'm no killer. I admit it's an amazing coincidence—if it's true that Colleen and Deb were both murdered—but strange things do happen in this crazy world."

"It's not a coincidence, is it, Mr. Rydberg?"

"It sure as hell is." I thought for a moment. "All right, maybe it's not a complete coincidence if you think about it the right way."

"And what is the right way?"

"Well, these two young women were out in public. They weren't at home, and, as far as I know, they weren't accompanied by friends or family. In a word, they were alone. And that means they were somewhat vulnerable—not just to me, but to anyone.

"They were both in a similar location: the Renaissance Festival. They had that in common with each other, not just with me. That suggests to me that someone was out there, stalking vulnerable women at the Ren Faire. There appears to have been a serial killer, but it isn't me. I just happened to hook up with the victims. I don't know how long DNA stays in the body, or when, or where, or how the murders occurred. Maybe he followed them home. Maybe he carjacked them in the parking lot and took them somewhere. I'm sure if there was a murder at the Festival, it would have been a big story. Word would have gotten around fast. It's a tight-knit group, those Ren Faire people. They travel from location to location together. You see what I'm getting at?"

"All right, Mr. Rydberg. You're saying this is all a giant misunderstanding based on the fact that you had sex with two murder victims shortly before they were killed."

"Yes, exactly. See, you never say *when* they were killed. You say 'shortly' after I was with them. What does that mean? An hour after we had sex? Four hours? Twelve? Twenty-four? Forty-eight?"

"It's all just an amazing coincidence."

"Come on, Lieutenant. I just explained this to you. It's not a pure coincidence. You must have a term for it. Propinquity. Two young women and their killer, or killers—all in one small area."

"Propinquity?"

"It means nearness in place or time. You know—like kids who marry their high school sweethearts. They marry them because they went to the same school and knew each other, not because they were the one person in the whole world who was 'meant' for them. Before online dating, propinquity was the main reason people fell in love and got married. That's what's going on here. Propinquity. People near each other. Crimes of convenience."

"So you're saying the killer was someone else at the Renaissance Festival."

"I'm saying it *could* have been. Based on propinquity, it's just as likely it was one of them as it was me. Look, I'm not accusing anyone, but it's a fact that some of those actors carried swords and daggers and things like that. They staged duels, swordfights. Maybe one of them was obsessed with knives. Maybe all that acting made him fantasize about actually doing it. The fact that they had weapons makes them more likely to be killers than me, if you want my opinion. I didn't have a sword or a dagger. I was just a poet in a fucking dress."

Brenner made a note in his file.

"Let me ask you this," said Thorsen. "Did you have sex with anyone else at the Renaissance Festival?"

Chapter Four

"Oh, shit. Now what?"

"I'm just asking a question."

"Don't tell me you have another file over there."

"Did you have sex with anyone else at the time of the Renaissance Festival?"

"At the time of the Renaissance Festival? Not at the Renaissance Festival? Now we're looking at a certain time frame?"

"Just answer the question."

"Why? Do you have more DNA?"

"Should we?"

"I don't know. I don't know what you have. That's what I mean about your being sneaky. You're not putting all your cards on the table."

"It's a simple question: Did you have sex with anyone else during this time period?"

"Not counting Diane, right? Because she's still alive? Okay. I had an encounter. Maybe this will prove my truthfulness, because if there's more DNA, it's going to show I'm being honest down to the last detail."

"Go ahead."

"All right. As I said, I didn't have a car. I always 'depended on the kindness of strangers' for rides to and from the festival. That's a little Tennessee Williams for you—Blanche DuBois in *A Streetcar Named Desire*: 'I have always depended on the kindness of strangers.' This is a little foggy to me, but I believe my college girlfriend, Cheryl, had two female friends who were going to the Renaissance Festival, and they gave me a ride. I don't believe Cheryl went with us. I have no memory of her being there, but she may have been. It makes sense that she would go, rather than just introduce me to her friends.

"I don't remember the one girl's name, but the driver's name was Tina. I don't know her last name. You could ask Cheryl."

Brenner made a note.

"Cheryl Harmon," I said. "She might remember. Both of her friends were attractive, as I recall. Tina had long dark hair; the other girl had light hair. I think the blonde was a little prettier. What I remember is not so much going there with them as much as coming home. You'll see why in a second. I'm ninety percent sure they were Cheryl's friends, but I might be confused. I might have hitchhiked home.

"Regardless, I was with these two young women—one named Tina—and they were going all the way to Saint Paul. They were going to take me home, but they wanted to stop at a nightclub on the way."

"Do you remember the name of the club?" asked Brenner.

"I'm going to say it was The Roadhouse or something like that. It was outside the Twin Cities, on the highway to Shakopee. At any rate, they wanted to go there because they wanted to see a band that was playing—the Lamont Cranston Band. There was another band that opened for them, The Daisy Dillman Band. The girls thought Daisy Dillman was okay, but they were really there to see Lamont Cranston.

"I didn't know either band, but I thought Daisy Dillman was great. They played country rock, kind of like the Eagles or the Allman Brothers. But they had this fantastic violinist. This guy was amazing. He'd shut his eyes and play a few chords, then break into these incredible solos.

"There were rumors that the great violin composer Paganini had made a pact with the Devil because his playing was unlike anything anyone had ever seen. That's how this guy struck me—possessed by some kind of spirit.

"At one time, I had season tickets to the Saint Paul Chamber Orchestra when Pinchas Zukerman was the director. Zukerman was a great violinist, but he had nothing on the guy in Daisy Dillman.

"Anyway, I figured it was better to sit through two shows and have a sure ride home than to take my chances hitchhiking. I really enjoyed the music. You know, I'd been listening to flutes and recorders every weekend for a month at the Ren Faire. I was sick of it. It was great to hear a beat. Not just hear it—feel it. And Daisy Dillman was tight. To this day, I say it was the best live performance I've ever seen, and I've seen some big bands. When Daisy Dillman signed a record deal, I rushed out and bought their album. It didn't quite capture the magic of the live performance, but it was still good."

"That's fine," said Thorsen. "Now, did you have sex with these women?"

"No. I remember that Tina dropped her friend off first. It seemed more logical to drop me off first, since it sounded like they lived near each other, but there was kind of a wink and a nod, like Tina wanted to be alone with me. If so, that was cool. I was attracted to her, but it was getting late. I mean, we'd stayed until the club closed at one or two in the morning.

"When we got to where I lived, I had Tina park in a service station on the main street, right below the little house—like a guest house—that Diane and I rented. I didn't want her to pull up close to the house because I was afraid the car would wake Diane up. The service station was closed. She turned off the engine. The details aren't that clear, but we must have started kissing. What I remember is that she opened my pants and began to give me a blow job.

"I felt very uncomfortable—not because of what she was doing, but because I was afraid Diane could see us from the bedroom window. If I'd had any brains, I would have just asked Tina to go to her place, but it was too late. Diane might have spotted us. I love sex, but getting a blow job in front of my live-in partner was cruel, even for me. I asked Tina to stop."

"Was she angry about that?"

"I don't remember. She might have been. I don't remember a lot after she stopped. I don't even remember zipping up my pants. I think I sneaked into the house. When I came into the bedroom, I was pretty sure Diane hadn't seen us from the window. She seemed to be asleep. Of course, later I got the third degree for coming home so late and my hair smelling like smoke—clubs allowed smoking back then, and Diane hated the smell of cigarette smoke. All I know is that she didn't find out about Tina."

"Did you ever see Tina again?"

"No."

"Talk to her by phone?"

"No."

"So you don't know what happened to her after you were with her?"

"No, but I know she left. Her car wasn't there the next morning."

"Did you leave with her?"

"No. Like I just said, I went inside the house that Diane and I rented."

"What did you mean about the DNA proving your truthfulness?" asked Brenner.

"What I meant is that if something happened to Tina, and if my DNA was on her, it wasn't inside her. If you found my DNA on her, it was from saliva on her lips or maybe her neck. Or maybe I left a hair or hairs on her clothing or possibly her skin. It definitely wasn't semen, because I had her stop. My DNA was not in her vagina. We didn't have sex."

"Did that enrage you?" asked Thorsen.

"Seriously, Lieutenant? Why do you keep doing that? I'm doing my best to tell you what happened. I'm not leaving anything out."

"Can you answer my question?"

"No. It didn't enrage me. I felt sorry for her, in a way. Not that I'm God's gift to women, but she obviously wanted to have sex that night. When I look back on it, it seems like the whole thing might have been a set-up, you know, for Tina and me to hook up. Cheryl thought I was good in bed. Maybe she bragged about me a little. I don't know. But no, I wasn't enraged—only embarrassed."

"Embarrassed about what?"

"Embarrassed that I wasn't man enough to go with her. To stand up for myself. To be strong and independent. In retrospect, Diane didn't deserve even the little bit of loyalty I showed that night. I wish I had gone with Tina. I wish I had fucked her brains out."

"Did you?"

"Once again, no. I didn't. I'm just saying I wish I had. I hate the person I was when I was with Diane. I was weak. She was domineering, but I didn't know how to stand up for myself. It took the marriage counseling we went through later for me to see my part in the relationship. I wasn't just a passive victim. I allowed myself to be bullied and manipulated. I had never learned how to cope with a person like Diane. She was manipulating, but I was 'manipulable,' as my therapist put it."

"I see. Did you take out your hatred for Diane on these girls?"

I took another sip of the coffee. It tasted good. "I see where you're coming from, Lieutenant Thorsen. It sounds a bit like a classic serial killer—dominated by someone and taking it out on someone else."

"Is that what you were doing?"

"No."

"Okay, Mark," said Brenner. "I hear the pain in your voice. I understand the burden you must be carrying. I can tell that you have feelings about all this. You'll feel much better if you just tell us everything. You won't have to hide anything anymore. Look, I get it. Diane pushed you around and made you feel like less than a man. She played on your weakness every day. You hate her, right?"

"Yeah. I probably do."

"Of course you do. Anyone would understand that. She was really on you about this Renaissance Festival. You wanted to strike back at her, but you couldn't do it. So you exploded with these girls. Maybe they said something that bothered you. Did they express disappointment about your premature ejaculation?"

"I don't remember. I don't think so."

"Did they laugh at you?"

"I don't remember that they did. I was probably pissed at myself for coming so fast, but I don't remember them saying anything."

"But let's be honest, Mark. You literally don't remember anything that happened after the sex act with any of these girls. You have no clear, independent recollection of anything, do you? It's as if you blacked out. It's as if you don't want to remember. Maybe they made fun of you. Maybe they laughed at you. They pushed your buttons, and you exploded at them. All that rage you felt for Diane came pouring out. Maybe you didn't plan to kill them, but you did."

I finished the coffee. “Do you have a restroom? I need to pee. It’s a bitch, getting old.”

“Sure,” said Brenner. “Follow me.”

He led me to a restroom. I really had to go, and I felt a lot better afterward.

Chapter Five

"Are we done here?" I asked when I returned to the room.

"Just a few more questions," said Thorsen. She looked at her notes. "You said that you didn't believe the victims were killed on the grounds of the Renaissance Festival. Is that right?"

"Yes."

"Why not?"

"Like I said, word travels fast. If a murder occurred at or near the Renaissance Festival, the people working there would have been talking about it. I was there every weekend. I never heard anything about any murders."

"You suggested that the killer might have carjacked the victims. What makes you think that?"

"It's logical, right? If someone spotted them at the Renaissance Festival—the festival being something they had in common—but they weren't killed there, then the killer had to either follow them to another location or else ride with them. If they rode with them, then it seems more likely they were carjacked than that they just gave some guy a ride."

"That's your propinquity theory."

"Yes."

"You seem like an uncommonly good guesser, Mr. Rydberg."

"How's that?"

"We never told you where the murders occurred, but you just told us."

"Another coincidence?" asked Brenner.

"I don't understand. What did I tell you?"

"Both victims were murdered in their cars," said Thorsen. The beginning of a smile creased the corner of her mouth.

I had to admit that looked suspicious. To me, it was just logic. Maybe it came from mapping out plotlines in my stories. You're always trying to create plausible cause and effect. They weren't killed at the festival, so it was logical that the killer followed them or abducted them. "Were they followed or carjacked?"

"You tell us."

"I don't know."

"Sure you do. You already said you didn't own a car."

"But you're assuming I did it!"

Brenner spoke up again. "If someone else did it, why did they abandon the cars within walking distance of the Snelling Avenue bus line—the very bus line that passes right below the house you were renting at the time? Is that just another coincidence?"

"That's right," said Thorsen. "The vehicles weren't abandoned near their homes, so they weren't followed home. And there was no damage to the vehicles to suggest they were forced off the road. In fact, the vehicles were carefully parked, and the parking brake was set."

"The wounds were inflicted from the passenger's side," said Brenner. "Everything points to a carjacking."

"Or a hitchhiker," said Thorsen, raising her eyebrows slightly.

"What I said is merely logic," I said. "Haven't you read Arthur Conan Doyle? Sherlock Holmes? They were just logical deductions. They had the Ren Faire in common, but they weren't killed there. The logical deduction is that someone followed them or rode with them. If they rode with them, it's likely they were carjacked."

"Logic and coincidence," said Brenner.

"Propinquity," I said. "It could be anyone from the Ren Faire, other than me. Dozens worked there, and thousands visited."

"But the DNA only points to one of them," said Thorsen.

I shook my head. This was going in circles. "And I have explained my DNA. In detail."

Thorsen narrowed her eyes. "You made up those stories about sex on the hillside and in the vendor booth, didn't you?"

I just looked at her.

"The sex wasn't consensual, was it? You raped those women in their cars."

"No! That's not true. It was totally consensual. They even initiated it—both times. And I never saw them in or near any cars. I didn't even know they had cars."

"Mark," said Brenner. "It will be much better for you if you start telling the truth."

"I am telling the truth. You know I am. You know I didn't just make up those stories."

"Let me ask you this," Thorsen interrupted. "Did you have sex with anyone else during this period?"

"I've already answered that question. I had sex with my partner, Diane, but she's still alive."

"What about later that year, or in subsequent years?"

"What do you mean?"

"Did you have sex with anyone other than Diane in the years that followed?"

"I don't see how that's relevant."

"We'll worry about the relevance. Did you?"

"Yeah, sure, lots of women. I'm on my third marriage. There were whole stretches between my marriages when I was single. I've had a lot of partners. What of it?"

"When did you leave the Twin Cities?"

"1988."

"Did you have sex with anyone in the Twin Cities, other than Diane, between the Renaissance Festival and 1988?"

It was a smart move to bring in a woman. If they wanted to turn up the heat, they were succeeding.

"Yes, Lieutenant Thorsen, I did. Diane and I got married in 1980, and we separated for a couple of years in 1986 and 1987, but we got back together. We had kids, you know? My son, Adam, and my daughter, Megan. So after getting marriage counseling, we got back together for the kids' sake. I had sex with a few women when we were separated, but I believe they're all alive. I'm Facebook friends with three of them, and there are a couple others I've seen who have Facebook accounts. They're all alive and well."

"All of them? You're sure about that? Are there any other partners from the Twin Cities that you might have been with but have lost track of?"

"I don't think I'm going to answer any more of your questions. I don't see what good it will do me. I've told you the truth about Colleen, Deb, and Tina, and you still think I killed them. I don't see what answering more questions will get me."

"Let me ask you this," said Thorsen. "Did you know a Julie Danner?"

Chapter Six

"Oh, no. Not Julie! Don't tell me she was murdered, too!"

"Why don't you tell us?"

"I don't know! Stop playing games with me. Did something happen to her?"

"I think you know," said Thorsen.

"I don't know a damn thing." I closed my eyes, leaned forward, and rested my head in my hands. I took another deep breath. "Did something happen to Julie?"

"She was murdered."

"Oh, no. Oh, God, no. Not Julie."

"Why don't you tell us about it."

"There's nothing to tell."

"How did you know her?"

"We worked together. As I told Detective Brenner, at the same time I was at the Ren Faire on weekends, I was working at a hat factory. It was located in downtown Minneapolis, one block off Hennepin Avenue, on Fifth Street. The Wyman Building. Eleven stories tall. My employer had the first, fifth, and ninth floors. We had a warehouse on the eleventh.

"Anyway, I was an assistant to the mechanic at the hat factory, so I worked on all the floors. I didn't work on the sewing machines. I'm not mechanically inclined. I'd just take them to the workshop and bring a replacement to the sewing line. Manual labor. Julie worked on the ninth floor. She didn't sew. She moved partially sewn caps from one seamstress to another to keep everyone busy.

"She was really beautiful—maybe the most beautiful woman I've ever seen in person. Long dark hair, deep blue eyes, flawless figure. You know how Elizabeth Taylor looked when she was young? That was Julie. Natural blush in her cheeks. High cheekbones. Just a gorgeous girl."

"When were you intimate with her?"

"I never said I was intimate with her."

"You were, though."

"Was I?"

"Yes."

I decided not to say anything.

"You had sex with her, right?" Thorsen prodded.

"I'm not going to answer that question."

"But you did."

I decided to follow my gut. It was a bit of a bluff, but I was sure I was right. "You have no evidence of that."

"We do."

"Bullshit."

"Why do you say that?"

"Because you don't."

"Why do you say that?"

"Because it's impossible. And may I add, for the record, the last time I saw Julie, she was alive and well."

"When was that?"

I decided to fuck with them for a change. I said nothing.

"May I go now?"

"Just a few more questions."

"No more questions. Review your video. I've told you everything I know. May I go?"

"I want to ask you another question about the first three murders, not about Julie Danner."

"All right. Go ahead."

"According to your propinquity theory, you think it's likely that someone else at the Renaissance Festival killed Colleen and Deborah, because they had access to knives, daggers, and swords. Is that correct?"

"Yes. It's a fact that some of them carried such weapons. And if I'm not wrong, I believe some vendors sold them there—fancy daggers and swords for cosplayers and wannabees."

"If you didn't kill these young women, how did you know they were killed with a combat knife or a dagger? The marks on the sides of the wounds indicate the weapon had a large hilt, possibly ornate—like a dagger you could get at the Ren Faire."

A gruesome image of Colleen flashed through my mind. It was too much to bear. Tears came.

"You did it, didn't you?" snapped Thorsen.

I shook my head. "No," I said. I took a deep breath. "No. I didn't. It's just that it's a shock. I didn't know how they were killed. I didn't want to know."

"Mr. Rydberg, you were correct when you said we know you are a writer. As a matter of fact, we have read your novels. The word *dagger* appears fifty-two times in your first novel and forty-seven times in your second. In your first novel, two people are killed with swords and one with a dagger. In your second, four people are killed—two with swords and two with daggers. In addition, a jail keeper holds a dagger to the throat of a woman under his control—a woman he plans to rape. At the end of the book, that woman's father fantasizes about avenging her death by stabbing her killer with a dagger."

Thorsen glanced at the folder she was holding. "Quote: 'He traced the dagger's blade with his fingertip. He would slice the king's heart in two. It would be over before the guards could end his own life. He only hoped he would live long enough to see the light go out of the king's eyes.'"

She looked up. "Is that what it's like, Mr. Rydberg? Watching the light go out of their eyes?"

"That's just a story. It takes place a thousand years ago. Swords and daggers were all they had."

"You enjoy killing, don't you?"

"No. Of course not. I put those scenes in there to raise the stakes in the stories. Life and death. If the stakes are lower, the reader gets bored."

"You thought you would never get caught, so you felt free to describe your murders. Isn't that true?" Thorsen was just barely controlling her anger.

"Look, I understand how it looks to you. The pieces of the puzzle seem to fit together. A fascination with daggers, victims who were stabbed, and of course the fact that I knew them—literally and biblically."

"Damn right it fits," Thorsen hissed. "And here's another thing that fits. We executed search warrants with your streaming services. You like serial killers, don't you?"

"What? No."

"You watch a lot of shows about them on Netflix and YouTube."

"A lot of people find serial killers interesting. That's why there are shows about them."

"But not everyone is obsessed with them."

"I'm not obsessed. I'm just interested."

"Do you know how many videos you've watched about Jack the Ripper?"

"I've watched a few. There's a guy on YouTube who does a whole series. It's called *The House of Lechmere.* He examines all the different theories."

"How many is it, Lieutenant?" asked Thorsen.

"Seventy-two," said Brenner. "Seventy-two videos about Jack the Ripper."

"You love Jack the Ripper, don't you, Rydberg?" asked Thorsen.

I met her eyes. My anger was rising. "No, I don't love Jack the Ripper."

"You admire him. He killed women. He slit their throats, just like you. But *he* never got caught."

"A lot of people are fascinated by Jack the Ripper. It's spawned a cottage industry. They call it 'ripperology.' I'm a writer, so I'm fascinated by facts and the interpretations of facts. I'm more interested in the theories than the murders."

"Sure you are." Thorsen closed her binder. "All right, Mr. Rydberg, you are free to go. Don't try to go anywhere. We'll be watching."

Brenner spoke up. "We'll process your DNA and see how that comes out. It will be up to the District Attorney to determine if there is enough evidence to charge you. But if I were you, I would get my affairs in order. You might be arrested at any time."

Chapter Seven

"So that's how I got here," I said to my cellmate, Leon Watson.

"I guess the DNA matched."

"Of course it did. I told them I had sex with the victims."

"They didn't charge you for the third girl, Tina?"

"No. The only evidence they had for that was my statement. She wasn't killed the night she gave me a ride home, and if there was any DNA, it was gone by the time she died, which apparently was a few days afterward. Her friend, the blonde, told the police she drove me home, which implicated me, but she was alive after dropping me off. Several people saw her over the next few days, so they didn't have anything tying me to the crime. Oh, they thought I did it, but they couldn't prove it. So they went with the other two."

"But how could they arrest you? The only evidence they had was your statement and your DNA. There ain't nothin' linking you to any crime."

"Actually, there was."

"What was that?"

"My ex-wife, Diane. They interviewed her before they interviewed me. She told them she'd noticed cuts and scratches on my hands, arms, and face when I came back from the Ren Faire a couple of times. Just outright lied. That was really important, because the prosecution said at trial that I got the marks when the victims fought back. Oh, and there was one more thing. The police reports said the victims had their panties removed. They found them in the car. That, along with my DNA, made it look like I raped them before I killed them."

"Is that what the rape kits showed?"

"Not exactly. They were inconclusive. The methods they used fifty years ago weren't as reliable as now. But they didn't clear me, either."

"What about the trial?" asked Watson.

"The trial? The trial was a joke. All circumstantial. No murder weapon. None of my DNA at the crime scenes. Nothing linking me to the murders—only to the sex."

"But that was enough."

"Yeah, it was enough. Well, that and the descriptions of killings in my books, my TV viewing history, my lack of an alibi for any of the murders, and Diane's statements. She testified at the trial."

"What did she say?"

"She said I had a history of physically abusing her."

"Did you?"

"No, I didn't. She did. She beat the shit out of me."

"How big was she?"

"Five-one, maybe a hundred-ten pounds. Small, but with a pit bull mentality. She didn't know when to stop. She used to hit me all the time. But I was taught never to hit a woman, so I just took it. Once she came up behind me with a wooden chair and hit me so hard the chair broke across my back. Another time I was sitting in a chair and she was standing in front of me. We were arguing, and then I stopped talking. I just sat there. That pissed her off, so she slapped me. Hard. I didn't say a thing. I just sat there. She slapped me again. Nothing. Again. Again. I started counting. She slapped me twenty-three times."

"Shit."

"The next day when I looked in the mirror, I could see her handprint on my face. She'd actually worn off layers of skin where she slapped me."

"Crazy."

"I know, right? Another time she hit me on the side of my head with her open hand. She busted my eardrum. It sounded like I was in a wind tunnel. The pain was incredible. I fell on the floor, holding my ear. 'What's the matter with you?' she said. She was laughing at me, like I was being a baby about it. A year later, I tried to go swimming with my kids, and the water got in my ear. Shit. It still hurt like hell."

"Did you hit her?"

"Only once, and that was with an open hand. We were arguing, and she started hitting me as usual—hitting, kicking. I put her in a bear hug and pinned her arms to her side. She kept kicking. I kept telling her to calm down. We were face-to-face, and she spit in my face. Some of her saliva went in my mouth."

"Nasty."

"Yeah. That was too much for me. Spit in my face. So I slapped her."

"Good for you. You tell that in court?"

"No, they didn't want me to testify. They said it would just become a 'he said, she said' situation. They didn't want me being cross-examined. They didn't want me talking about my escapades with the other women. So she sat up there, lying under oath, telling all kinds of stories about me that weren't true."

"What about motive?"

"Motive!" I laughed. "They had a couple shrinks testify about my transferring my hate for Diane onto the victims. They said my lack of remorse was from the suppression of the memories. I didn't act like a killer because I didn't know I killed. I suppressed the memory of it."

"How long was the jury out?"

"Not long. Juries today put all their faith in DNA. I was with the victims. They were killed. So I must have killed them."

"But you didn't."

"No, Man, I didn't. At least, I don't think I did. Those psychiatrists. The lack of memories. I don't know. Maybe it's true. Maybe I killed them and blocked it out. Maybe the truth is coming out in my stories."

"Bullshit."

"What do you mean?"

"Man, you didn't kill nobody."

"Why do you say that?"

"C'mon, Man," he drawled. "I know what a killer's like. It ain't you."

"Thanks. I guess."

"Only one thing you did right."

"What's that?"

"You pleaded not guilty."

"Is that important?"

"Yeah. It means you can get a new trial."

"A new trial? Based on what?"

"Based on new evidence, Motherfucker."

I laughed. "What the fuck are you talking about?"

"Man, you s'posed to be smart. You write all them books. You tell a good story. Like now. That story you told me was all right."

"Yeah?"

"Yeah. But it was bullshit."

"What you mean?"

"I mean it's got holes in it. Big holes. The holes in your story so big I could drive my old beer truck right through 'em."

"What kind of holes?"

"You'd like me to tell you, wouldn't you?"

"Of course."

"Well, why the fuck should I?"

"I don't know. To help me?"

"You in here a month, and you want me to help you get out! I been here ten years. Why should I help you out? Maybe after ten or fifteen years, I'll help you."

"You're just bullshitting me."

"Oh, wow," said Watson. "You gonna use reverse psychology on me now? And I'm so dumb I gonna fall for it. That what you think?"

"No, Man." I smiled. "It's all right. I wouldn't help me, either. I got myself into it. Or my dick did."

Leon laughed. "You love that pussy."

"Yeah, Man."

"You ever go black?"

"Yeah, I did. She was one of those girls in the Twin Cities I said I'm still in touch with on Facebook. We used to ride the bus together. We got off at the same stop, way out in the suburbs. She went left, to Control Data, and I went right, to

Land O' Lakes. Eventually, we started meeting for lunch. She was nineteen and had a killer body."

"How old were you?"

"At that point, I was twenty-seven."

"And what happened?"

"I guess it was obvious I was attracted to her. One night, when Diane was out of town, I had her over. One thing led to another and we had sex. It was great."

"Look at you, makin' it with a sister."

"Yeah. It was amazing."

"Didn't you want to cut her?"

"Fuck you, Watson."

"Man, I'm just playin' with you. I know you're not a killer. You're like MJ." He made his voice high and soft. "'I'm a lover, not a fighter.'"

"'The Girl Is Mine.' I get it. Anyway, it's probably just as well I don't get out."

"What you mean?"

"You know, I'm seventy. Overweight. I don't have that long to live. I've lived my life. I've done everything I wanted to do. I accomplished more than I ever expected to. I'm okay with being in here. I can still write, if I want. But if I get out, think of the victims' families. Right now, they think justice has been done. The murderer is paying for his crimes. They probably wish Minnesota had a death penalty, but at least they have the comfort of knowing I'm behind bars. If I got out on a technicality, they'd lose that. The wounds would open again. It would rob them of that peace."

"See that, right there? That's how I know you ain't no killer."

"Maybe. I see your point. I'm not a psychopath."

"Anyway, they're not gonna feel bad."

"No?"

"No, Man."

"Why not?"

"'Cuz you're gonna bring the real killer to justice."

"The real killer. Like O.J.?"

"Yeah, except you're really innocent."

"You think so, huh?"

"I know you ain't no killer."

"All right, who's the real killer?"

"Shit," Leon drawled. "I can't believe how motherfuckin' dumb you are."

"What do you mean?"

"Fuck. I should just sit here and let you work it out."

"Yeah. I suppose you should."

"Why? You think I got no heart? You think I enjoy watchin' innocent people sit in prison?"

"I didn't mean that. I just mean I see your point of view. You help me out, but who's helping you out?"

"Right."

"Hey, Leon. Look, Man, if you can get me out of here, I'll help you any way I can. I'll visit you, I'll discuss your case with a lawyer. I won't forget about you."

"Yeah?"

"Sure. Whatever I can do."

"I believe you. That's the kind of guy you are. Not a killer."

"Why do you keep saying that? Can you just tell me that much?"

"Okay. I'll tell you."

Chapter Eight

"You say that maybe you killed these girls, but you don't remember it. That right there don't make no sense."

"Why not?"

Watson leaned back on his bed, bracing himself on his elbows. "It's like this. You admit you got a temper. Okay, let's say one of these girls made fun of you. Let's say she laughed at you, and it made you mad. Suddenly, you don't see that girl no more. You see your ex-wife, or you see all women who piss you off. You explode. Now let me ask you this: when you had sex with these girls, did you have a knife on you?"

"No. No, I didn't."

"There you go. Their whole theory is you got so mad you lost control and cut them. But if that's true, it'd be like when you slapped your ex-wife. It'd happen right then. Boom. You'd kill that redhead on the hill, and you'd kill the girl in the tight dress during that rainstorm. Now, maybe you decide to move the bodies later. But that ain't what the police say. They say you killed 'em *in* their cars. That don't fit with you killin' in a rage. Don't you see? To kill 'em in the car that way, you gotta get angry but not explode. You gotta wait till later. Now you gotta follow 'em to their cars, or get a ride with 'em, then kill 'em. But you ain't in a rage anymore. Too much time passed.

The rage is over, Man. If you kill 'em in the car, you're doin' it cold blooded. You think you wouldn't remember that?"

"I see. That's a good point."

"Fuck yeah, it's a good point. I shouldn't be in here. I should be your goddamn lawyer. Shit."

"Yeah, I can see blacking out for a few minutes, forgetting what happened, but in some cases the murder was a day later."

"Right. And there's another thing."

"What's that?"

"Oh Man, you gettin' excited now. You think Ol' Leon gonna spring you outta this motherfuckin' joint."

"Look, Leon. This shit's been hanging over me for two years now. It's been torture. This is the first glimmer of hope I've had."

"See, here's the thing: You can't do a damn thing for yourself till you know for sure you ain't the killer."

"Yeah."

"All right. Leon gonna give you another thing to think about. See, you've never killed no one, so you think it's easy."

"Not necessarily."

"No? But you think you can wake up the next day without a scratch on you and without a drop of blood anywhere on your clothes, and yet you cut a girl's throat. Shit."

I thought about it for a minute.

Leon went on. "You don't remember changin' clothes. Or washin' blood out of 'em. And you know for damn sure if your ex-wife saw blood on your clothes she'd be all over your ass." He pitched his voice high: "'What did you do? Fuck a girl on her period?'"

"That's true."

"But there's no blood on your clothes because you never cut those girls, Man. Come on, Dude. You s'posed to be smart. You're actin' like a fool. See, you lettin' the police get in your head. You be thinkin' 'someone had to kill those girls, so maybe it's me.' But it can't be you. Think!"

"You make a good point."

"'Make a good point.' Fuck. Listen to you. You should be mad, Motherfucker. You're in here for nothin', and the real killer's out there, roamin' around free. 'Make a good point.' Fuck you."

"Look, Leon. I'm processing all this, all right? I gotta think about this shit."

"Yeah, you think. You think about it till you die in here."

"Are these the holes in the case you were talking about? The ones you could drive through?"

"What? You want more outta me?"

I got up and went over to his bed and sat next to him. Nobody had tried to help me since this all began. Now someone was. "Please, Leon. If you know anything that can help me, please tell me. I want to understand. It's not just prison. I want to know the truth." My voice cracked.

"It's okay. I understand. This shit ain't easy."

"What else do you see that I'm not seeing?"

"Motive, Man. You ain't got no motive."

"What do you mean?"

"I mean those girls never said nothin' bad to you. That's just some prosecutor's fucked-up story. Those bitches dug you, Man. They wanted to fuck you. Maybe it wasn't the best fuck of their lives, but I'm sure it was a lot better than you think.

"And think about this: they pursued you; you didn't pursue them. Tell me, you ever hear of a serial killer who didn't pursue their victims? Who waited for them to come to him? Man, those bitches wanted to get with you. And they did. You think that was bad for them? No, Man. It was good for them.

"Don't you see? They didn't make fun of you. So you didn't have any reason to get mad. It's like you said. It was a beautiful thing. So what motive you have? The only motive—now hear me, Motherfucker—the *only* motive is if you're a cold-blooded psychopath. You know, Ted Bundy, Richard Gacy—"

"Charles Lechmere."

"Who?"

"Jack the Ripper. The guy whose YouTube videos I watch believes Lechmere was Jack the Ripper."

Watson looked at me out of the corner of his eye. "I don't know 'bout you. Maybe you're psycho, after all."

I smiled. "All right, Leon. Let me see if I can guess where you're going. If I don't kill in a rage, then I'm a psychopath, and if I'm a psychopath…" I thought for a minute. "If I'm a psychopath, I don't stop killing after three girls."

"Bingo."

"So, if I didn't kill them, who did?"

"Shit, Man. Do I have to draw you a motherfuckin' picture? For fuck sake. Use your fuckin' brain."

"I don't know. I know you're right about all this, but that puts me back to square one. Someone at the Renaissance Festival?"

"Nope."

"Why not?"

"The fourth girl. The other one they didn't charge you with, 'cuz they didn't have nothin' on you. They didn't have DNA, right?"

"Right."

"But you fucked her, right?"

"Yeah, I did. How did you know?"

"Shit."

"Okay, so what?"

"See, that fourth girl fucks up your Renaissance Festival theory."

"Yeah. So what's the solution?"

"What's that word you use? Pro—"

"Propinquity?"

"Yeah. Propinquity."

"What do you mean? You just said the killer wasn't at the Renaissance Festival."

"Dude, let me ask you this: Who knew you fucked those girls?"

"Nobody. Only me and the girls."

"Bullshit."

"Why bullshit?"

"Man, how many people in the world? Seven billion? And outta seven billion people, only two people could possibly give a fuck about you havin' sex with those girls."

"You mean—"

"I mean Bitch did it."

I stopped to ponder what he was saying.

He continued. "She's the only person with a motive. She's the one."

"But that's impossible."

"How come it's impossible?"

"She wasn't anywhere near the Renaissance Festival."

"How do you know that?"

"She was at home."

"Did you see her at home?"

"No."

"Did you call her at home?"

"No. We didn't have a phone, believe it or not."

"So you don't know where the fuck she was."

"No, I guess I don't."

"So here's how it is. She followed you to the Renaissance Festival. She blended in with the crowd. She watched you. As long as you're a good boy, no problem. But when she sees you go off with the redhead, she follows you. She gets close enough to see what's goin' on. And that's it. She buys a dagger at one of the booths and, when the redhead's leavin', she asks for a ride. She says her car's broke down and she needs a ride to the first gas station or whatever. No one had cell phones back then. She convinces the girl to let her in the car. She's small, right? She looks harmless.

"Somewhere along the way, she has the redhead pull over, and boom! She reaches over and slits her throat. When she's dead, she removes the panty to make it look like a man done it—like you done it, 'cuz she knows you fucked her that day.

She moves over into the driver's seat, drives to a place near her bus line, drops the car, hops on a bus, and gets to the house before you do.

"Now, all you're thinkin' about is that you had sex with another girl and you're just hopin' she don't find out. You're not even lookin' at her.

"Anyway, she gets rid of her bloody clothes. When she gets home, she takes a shower. If she has any scratches, you don't ask about 'em. All you're thinkin' about is not gettin' caught for what you done. You don't suspect her of a damn thing."

"I had no reason to be suspicious because I didn't know that anything had happened."

"Right. And she acts pissed off at you for bein' late or whatever, so you don't have sex. You don't see her naked. You don't know what cuts or scratches she got."

"Right."

"And the second girl, same thing. She watches you talk with her. She sees you go into the booth. Maybe she looks inside or just listens. She follows that girl out the next day, tells her sob story, gets a ride, boom. Revenge. Rinse and repeat."

"But the third girl?"

"Yeah, now that was a little different. She saw you from the window and pretended to be asleep when you come in.

But she already wrote down the license number. Somehow she tracks down the car. Maybe she calls your old college girlfriend and asks for her friend's phone number. Maybe she makes up a story that you lost your wallet and she wonders if you left it in her car. Maybe she knows someone at the police. Somehow, she meets up with that girl and pretends she need a ride. Same MO."

"I guess it's possible."

"Possible? No, Man, it's real. 'Cuz you didn't kill 'em, and no one else had a motive. Look, you don't know what that bitch was doin' when you at work, makin' the fuckin' hats. Maybe she's here, maybe she's there. You don't know where the fuck she's at or what she's doing."

"Okay, but the last one. Julie. How do you explain that one?"

"Yeah, that's a little harder. I don't know when you have sex."

"I called her one time when Diane was out of town. She drove over to my house. She went home that night."

"You called her?"

"Yeah."

"You had her number somewhere?"

"In my address book."

"You have a little black book?"

"No, red. It was a pocket calendar with a place for addresses in the back."

"So Bitch checks it when she get back from outta town. She sees the number, makes a call, talks to the girl, says she wants meet. They meet somewhere, and, when she's sure she had sex with you—"

"She says she needs a ride to the bus stop or somewhere."

"That's it."

"Wow. Your name should be Holmes, not Watson."

"Like the movie, right? I saw it. They played it here. Everyone calls me Dr. Watson."

"Well, in this case you're Holmes, and I'm Watson."

"Yeah. And maybe you're gonna write it all down, how Leon Watson sprung you outta the joint."

"Right. So the killing stops because I stop playing around. Diane isn't a psychopath. She's just jealous. Insanely jealous."

"And she stops 'cuz you get a divorce, right?"

"Yeah." I looked down at my hands. "Let's say it's all true."

"It's all true."

"All right. How can I prove it?"

"C'mon, Man. Do I gotta do everything for you?

Chapter Nine

"Let me think. No one saw her, except for her victims. Or no one noticed her, even if they saw her get in the cars. The only tricky part was dumping the car and not getting noticed on the bus."

"Who's gonna notice her on a bus?" asked Leon.

"Yeah, it was nighttime for the first two. Only a few people on the bus. She probably took a coat or a shawl to cover up."

"Anyway, if someone noticed her, who's gonna remember that now?"

"No one."

"No. Fucking. One. But you were gettin' warm there for a second."

"I was?"

"Kinda."

I put on a fake British accent. "I believe I've got it, Holmes."

"Let's see."

"It's not the coming home, it's the going there. How did she get from Saint Paul to Shakopee?"

"No, Man. That's not it. That's good, but that's not it. There ain't no records now, fifty years later, even if she rent a car and use a credit card to do it. No, Man, it's much simpler."

I tried to think about how she slipped up. I couldn't get it. "I give up."

Watson smiled.

"Think back to the trial. What did you say?"

"I said they had my DNA and the jury believed that linked me to the crimes."

"What did you say they didn't have?"

"They didn't have anything that put me at the crime scenes."

"That's it."

"I still don't get it."

"Look, Man, the police say your DNA ain't in the cars. But they never said there's *no* DNA in the cars."

"You mean they might have collected Diane's DNA from one of the crime scenes, but they never matched it."

"Now you're thinkin' straight! I knew you had it in you."

"So if she left anything behind—a hair, blood, anything—the police assumed it was from the victim's friend or acquaintance because it didn't match mine, or maybe didn't match a male."

"Keep goin'."

"So if we could get them to test Diane's DNA, then they might find it matches the crime-scene DNA. Do you think they would test her?"

"Hell no. They got their killer and they already locked him up."

"So what good is any of this?"

"I'll tell you why. First, you gotta know for sure you ain't the guilty one. That's important, Man. You gotta believe you're innocent. Otherwise, your thinkin' is fucked up. Okay, now you believe it. Now, how can you catch the killer?"

"I don't know. How?"

"Easy. You said you have a son and a daughter with the Bitch, right?"

"Yeah."

"That's it. You test their DNA. If it comes out close to anything in the cars, then you've got reasonable cause to test the Bitch."

My kids. Why hadn't I thought of that?

Chapter Ten

"Hi, Daddy!"

"Hi, Megan. How are you doing?"

"I'm doing okay."

"How was your trip?"

"Not bad. A little bumpy coming into Minneapolis, but it was okay. What about you? How are you doing in there? What's it like?"

"It's all right. I have a really cool cellmate. Nice guy. In fact, he's the reason I asked you to fly up here."

"What do you mean?"

"I was talking to him about my case, and he thinks there are big holes in it."

"He does?"

"Yeah. You know the part about how I supposedly flew into a rage and killed those women? He makes a good point. He says if I did that, I would have killed them immediately. But that's not what they say happened. They said I followed them to their cars and killed them later. So how could I be in a rage that long? Rage is instantaneous—unless I'm some kind of psychopath, which I'm not."

"Okay," Megan said. She sounded skeptical.

"And if I didn't fly into a rage, then there's no motive. If we didn't fight, why would I kill them? What's the motive? And if I have no motive, then the only explanation is that I'm a psychopath. Leon—my cellmate—doesn't think the women did anything to make me mad. He thinks everything was good with them. He makes another good point: I didn't pursue them. They pursued me. Why would they be mad at me? And why would I be mad at them? It doesn't make any sense."

"All right. But what does this have to do with me?"

"I'm getting there. I'm sorry, but it's important to understand—really understand—that I'm innocent. Sometimes I even wondered about it myself. You know, the whole blackout thing, the supposed repression of memories. But if there was no fight, and no rage, then there was no blackout."

"I guess I see your point."

"You don't think I did it, do you?"

"No."

"And you don't want me to be in here for a crime I didn't commit, do you?"

"No."

"Wouldn't it be better if the real killer was here instead of me?"

"Of course. But I still don't know why you want me here. I wasn't even alive then."

"I know. I'm sorry. I don't want to put you in the middle of this. But I was wondering if you would allow my defense team to take a sample of your DNA."

"For what?"

"I'm not going to lie to you. There are only two people in the world who would have cared if I had sex with those young women. I was one. Your mom is the other."

Megan laughed. "You think Mom is the killer?"

"She's the only one with a motive. The only person in the whole world."

"But how?"

"Look, I've thought it through. It's possible, okay? But that's beside the point. The question right now is only whether or not you'll help me. I want you to let my lawyers do a cheek swab to collect your DNA. If there wasn't any DNA in the cars, or if the DNA from the crime scenes isn't close to yours, then your mom is in the clear. And she would never have to know you tried to help me. That's why I'm asking you directly. That's why I brought you here, rather than trying to get a court order to get her DNA. If you give us yours voluntarily, and it's a close match to something at the crime scenes, then at least I could get a court to reopen my case. If there's no match, it's no big deal. No one has to know."

"I don't know, Daddy. It seems kind of sketchy."

"It's not sketchy. You're not accusing your mom of anything. It's not your theory. It's not your idea to come here.

"All I'm asking is that you give us a sample of your DNA. Then you can just forget about it. Just think about this whole trip as one of your dad's crazy ideas."

"But what if it matches?"

"If it matches, it's new evidence, and a judge might order a new trial."

"But what about Mom?"

"If it matches, she'll have an opportunity to explain how her DNA got there. There might be an innocent explanation. I don't know. I wasn't there. I just know that I'm innocent. And I don't want my family, my friends, or the world to remember me as a killer."

"I don't know."

"Megan, it's about right and wrong. Guilt and innocence. It's about justice. You have a chance to play a meaningful role in letting the truth be known. Not many people have that chance. Play your part, and let the chips fall where they may. You're only responsible for doing your part."

"All right, Daddy. What do I do?"

"Just walk through those doors. My lawyer is out there. Tell her you consent to a buccal swab. Simple as that."

"Okay, Daddy. I'll do it. I love you."

Chapter Eleven

"Rydberg!"

It was the guard we jokingly called Smiley.

"Yeah, what is it?"

"Come with me."

"This might be it," said Watson.

My heart jumped at the idea. I took a deep breath. It probably wasn't what I was hoping for. One foot in front of the other.

When I entered the visiting area, I saw my lawyer smiling.

"You look happy," I said as I sat down.

"I am," she said. "The DNA results came back. We compared your daughter's DNA to the crime-scene DNA, and we have a couple of matches—a hair in Colleen Malone's car and blood in Deborah Jorgenson's. The police got a sample of your ex-wife's DNA from a glass at a restaurant, and it's a perfect match."

"So what's next?"

"We already filed for post-conviction relief, and the judge granted it. The judge didn't overturn the conviction, because the DNA doesn't conclusively prove your innocence. It does, however, provide evidence for an alternate theory of the crime that could create reasonable doubt. In light of that, the judge has ordered a new trial."

"That's fantastic! Thank you so much for following up with this."

"It's our pleasure. We want to see justice done."

"Do you think a jury will believe me?"

"I do. Remember how, at your trial, your ex-wife said she had never met or even seen the victims? This evidence proves she was lying about that. And if she was lying about that, a jury isn't going to believe her testimony about seeing scratches on you or about a history of physical abuse. At least, they shouldn't. We'll drive that point home. She's not credible. Even better, this explains why she would lie about you. She was deflecting suspicion away from herself. Her testimony really hurt your case in the first trial."

"Yeah."

"People understand jealousy and revenge. They may hate you for cheating on your girlfriend, but they won't convict you of murder if you weren't there and she was."

"What about her? Do you think they're going to arrest her?"

"They already have."

"They have?"

"Yes. They brought her in for questioning. They asked her again about knowing the victims, and again she denied ever seeing them. When they confronted her with the DNA evidence, she asked for a lawyer."

"I guess that didn't look good."

"No. Especially since the DNA proved she was lying."

"Is there enough evidence to convict her?"

"They have motive—jealousy and revenge for the victims' affairs with you. They have opportunity: they know she was in the vehicles where the murders occurred. And they have means. They don't have the murder weapon, but a knife or dagger is something she could conceal and use in a surprise attack. When you put that together with her deceptiveness and her attempt to frame you, well, it all fits together. Her team may argue that you did it together, or you put her up to it, but that's far-fetched."

"I hope they convict her—not for my own satisfaction, but so the victims' families can feel justice was done."

"Yes."

"Speaking of justice, I wanted to ask you for a favor."

"What is it?"

"My cellmate, Leon Watson. Would you be willing to take a look at his case? Maybe meet with him and get his side of the story?"

"Leon Watson?"

"Yeah. He's a great guy. He's the one who figured all of this out. I promised I would help him with his case."

"But the DA had a mountain of evidence against Leon Watson. We looked into it. They had his fingerprints at the crime scene, they recovered the murder weapon from his house, and they had eyewitnesses who saw him fleeing the scene. Leon Watson pleaded guilty."

"Oh. I didn't know that. Who did he kill?"

"His ex-wife."

Meet the Author

Cal Rydell is an copywriter by day and a novelist after dark. For a short time in the 1970s, he supported himself as a street poet. *The Ren Faire Murders* marks his crime fiction debut.

www.ingramcontent.com/pod-product-compliance
Lightning Source LLC
LaVergne TN
LVHW050938080826
845145LV00004B/1310

* 9 7 8 0 9 8 3 9 8 5 0 5 1 *